This Little Tiger book belongs to:

_____

_____

_____

*For Louis*
~ C W

*For Nina, my god-daughter*
~ A E

LITTLE TIGER PRESS
An imprint of Magi Publications
1 The Coda Centre, 189 Munster Road, London SW6 6AW
www.littletigerpress.com

First published in Great Britain 2009
This edition published 2009

A CIP catalogue record for this book is available from the British Library

Printed in China

2 4 6 8 10 9 7 5 3 1

# The Magical Snowman

Catherine Walters

*Illustrated by* Alison Edgson

LITTLE TIGER PRESS
London

It was a clear, sparkling winter's day and Little Rabbit had been busy all morning, heaping snow to make a snowman.

"That's lovely, Little Rabbit," said Daddy. "Could you finish it later though? I need you to find some berries for our tea."

"Snowman will be sad if I leave him now," Little Rabbit said.

"He'll be fine," said Daddy gently. "He is just a snowman. He isn't real."

"He *is* real!" said Little Rabbit. "Of course he's real! He's my friend!"

Daddy smiled as he gave Little Rabbit a kiss. "Don't go too far," he said.

"I won't!" said Little Rabbit.

"Mmm, one for the basket and one for me," he sang as he skipped down the lane. Soon his paws were sticky with purple juice.

Little Rabbit was having
so much fun . . .

he hardly noticed the snow
begin to fall.

A robin flitted ahead of
him and he followed it . . .

dancing through the drifting
snowflakes and bare trees.

Then the robin flew away. Little Rabbit stopped and looked around. He wasn't sure which way he had come. The swirling snow made everything look strange.

"What will I do?" he cried. "How will I get home?"

As if in answer, a soft light sparkled through the trees. Smiling through the falling snow was his very own Snowman!

"I *knew* you were real!" said Little Rabbit.
"But, Snowman, I was all on my own."
"Not all alone," smiled Snowman.
"I was there too, little friend. I was always
there for you."

Snowman dusted flakes from
Little Rabbit's fur and lifted
him on to his shoulders.
 "I'll take you home," he said.
"Hold on tight!"

They whizzed down the hill . . .

WHOOOOOOOOOSH!

and landed in a snowy heap
by a frozen stream.

"Here we go!" Snowman laughed as he held Little Rabbit's paw.

The world whisked by in a shimmer of silver frost. It felt as if they were flying.

"I'm coming home, Daddy!" Little Rabbit called.

WHEEEEEEEEEEEE!

Suddenly, Snowman skidded to a halt at the bottom of a hill.

"We'll have to walk now," he said, as he swung Little Rabbit into his soft arms.

"Are we nearly there yet?" yawned Little Rabbit.

"Not far now," said Snowman.

Meanwhile, Daddy Rabbit was hurrying through the whirling snow. He was very worried and he shivered in the icy wind.

"Little Rabbit!" he called. "Little Rabbit! Where are you?"

"Daddy!" cried Little Rabbit, when he heard his call. He leapt from Snowman's arms and bounded up the garden.

Daddy Rabbit swept him up and hugged him tight.

"Thank goodness you're safe!" he said. "I was so worried about you, all alone."

"I wasn't alone," said Little Rabbit. "Snowman
took care of me."

"Oh did he now?" Daddy chuckled.

Snowman stood quietly in the winter darkness.
Little Rabbit smiled at him. And he saw Snowman
was smiling too.

# More magical reads from
# Little Tiger Press

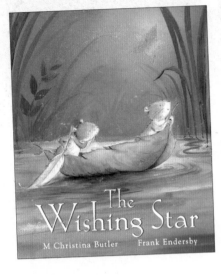

The Wishing Star
M Christina Butler · Frank Endersby

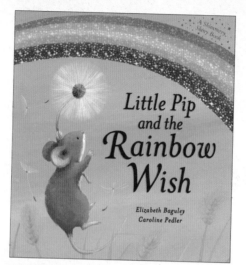

Little Pip and the Rainbow Wish
Elizabeth Baguley · Caroline Pedler

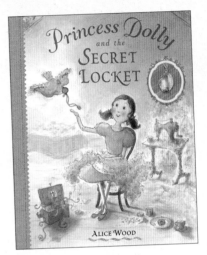

Princess Dolly and the SECRET LOCKET
ALICE WOOD

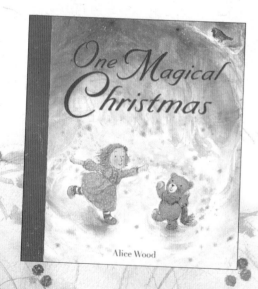

One Magical Christmas
Alice Wood

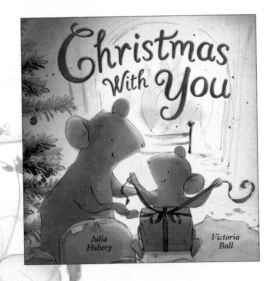

Christmas With You
Julia Hubery · Victoria Ball

One Winter's Night
Claire Freedman · Simon Mendez

For information regarding any of the above titles
or for our catalogue, please contact us:
Little Tiger Press, 1 The Coda Centre,
189 Munster Road, London SW6 6AW
Tel: 020 7385 6333  Fax: 020 7385 7333
E-mail: info@littletiger.co.uk  www.littletigerpress.com